BROWN SUGAR

A ROSEVILLE NOVELLA

D. ROSE

Editor: Tamara Lewis

Cover Image by Deji Akinyele on Unsplash

Cover Design: Roseville Designz

Poetry & Prose by Monét from *Joy Comes in the Morning*

STAY CONNECTED

Text **Rosebud** to **345345** to subscribe to my mailing list!

Join my facebook group for discussions and giveaways here: **The Rosebush**

Follow me on social media:

facebook.com/AuthorDRose
twitter.com/authordrose
instagram.com/whoisdrose

THE PLAYLIST

Available on iTunes: https://apple.co/2JWmCS8

SYNOPSIS:

Shiloh Hurston, a 27-year-old bank teller, and poet, is left piecing the remnants of her heart back together after ending a volatile and unsatisfying relationship. During her sabbatical from love, she finds healing in performing poetry at Ray's, a lounge located in the small town of Roseville. What started out as an escape turned into a secret admiration for another performer and crowd favorite, Marquis Kent.

Marquis Kent, a 28-year-old carpenter, and reformed preacher's kid, is desperately in need of a fresh start, and moving from his hometown to Roseville was the first step to a new life. He too finds relief in performing acoustic covers of his favorite songs at Ray's. His sultry voice paired with his southern charm made him a crowd favorite, including the person he least expected—Shiloh.

To Marquis, Shiloh is the perfect woman who has it all together—a woman clearly out of his league. To Shiloh, Marquis is just another heartbreak waiting to happen, but she can no longer resist the temptation...

A serendipitous encounter opens their eyes to the realization that they have more in common than what meets the naked eye. But are they willing to put their apprehensions aside and explore what could be?

AUTHOR'S NOTE

Roseville: a small predominately black town located in Maryland, USA. This town may be small, but black love & black businesses are alive and thriving…

Note: Please keep in mind this a novella (about 17k words) the main characters **will** have a HFN (happy for now) ending, and will be mentioned in subsequent projects. The minor characters mentioned in this novella will have their own stories in the future ;)!

Welcome to Roseville & Happy reading!
-D.

BROWN SUGAR

CONTENTS

Chapter 1 1
Chapter 2 12
Chapter 3 21
Chapter 4 32
Chapter 5 47
Chapter 6 59
Epilogue 67

Thank You! 73
Acknowledgments 75
Also by D. Rose 77

One truism in life, my friend...when that jones come down, it be a mothaf**ka.

- LOVE JONES, 1997.

CHAPTER 1

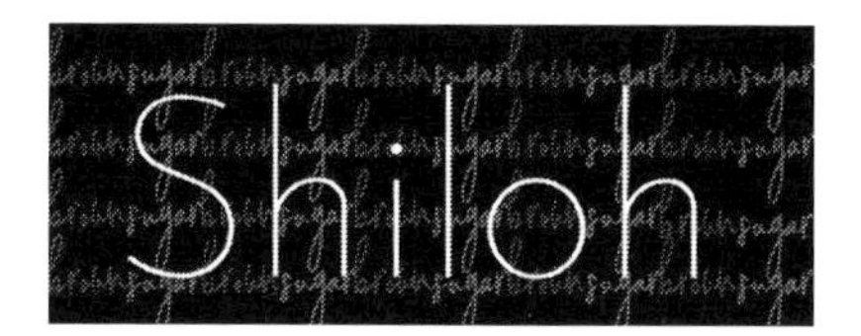

ANOTHER DAY, another dollar, but thank God it was *finally* Friday. I sighed in relief as I jotted down the final count of my drawer before turning to my coworker and friend, Ellie. She was babbling about her upcoming date with her husband, Jaime. Since she'd gotten married, her use of the word *husband* had increased significantly. But I couldn't even be mad. If I reconnected with my childhood crush and got married within a year, I'd talk about him all the time too.

Since I started working at Brickston Bank two years ago, Ellie had been adamant about being married by the time she was twenty-five. Luckily for her, it worked out. At that age, I thought I met "the one," but I learned the hard way he wasn't the man I thought he was. Since then, marriage was the furthest thing from my mind, and so was a serious relationship. The way my dating life was going, I'd be lucky if I was married before thirty, which was only three short years away.

While Ellie shared the details of her date tonight, I smiled and nodded. The way she lit up when she talked about Jaime made my heart swell. As sweet as Ellie was, she deserves all the happiness in the world. Her skin flushed as she showed me the flowers he sent her today. Every Friday for the past year, he sent her calla lilies, and every time she acted surprised. It was *disgustingly* cute.

"So how was your date?" she asked finally changing the subject, but honestly, I'd rather listen to her talk about Jaime.

"It was…" I paused. "Interesting to say the least."

Last night I went on a date with a guy I met on a dating app. What started as something to do when I was bored, turned into me swiping right. After my last relationship, I promised myself I would play the field and not focus solely on one man. I had a bad habit of putting all my eggs in one basket and was left heartbroken and looking foolish.

Ellie raised her brow and sighed. "What was wrong with him?"

"He was trying so hard to impress me that he ended up boring me. All night he went on and on about his career as a financial advisor." I rolled my eyes before continuing, "Once I shared that I too work in the finance industry he took that as an opportunity to talk about stocks, bonds, investing...all things I didn't necessarily want to talk about on a first date. You know?"

She nodded with a frown. "Yeah, I understand, Shi.

Don't get discouraged though. I'm sure your Prince Charming is closer than you think."

I smiled at her innocence. Ellie was truly a hopeless romantic, and it was adorable at times.

"Anyway," I said, changing the subject. There was no one even remotely close to being my *Prince Charming*

"What are you doing tonight?" she asked with wide eyes.

I hesitated before telling her the truth. "I'm going to an open mic night not too far from here."

I'd been going to *Ray's,* a swanky lounge that held open mic nights every Friday night, for almost a year now. It was located in Roseville, a small town about 20 miles north of Washington, D.C. One night, I stumbled upon this cute little town when I got lost coming back from visiting a friend in Philly. Everything about this town made me feel magical.

"Oh, the same open mic night you go to every week, but won't invite your dear friend? It's because I'm White isn't it?"

"What? No." I laughed. "I'm not comfortable sharing my poetry with friends and family yet."

And that was the God's honest truth. It took years for me to even reach a place where I wanted to share my poetry with anyone.

I grabbed her shoulder. "When I'm ready, you'll be the first to know."

"I hope that day is soon. I'm dying to hear how

talented my Shi is." She pinched my cheeks and laughed.

After we retrieved our things, our manager and the security guard walked us to the door. While we walked to our cars, Ellie showed me the house that she and Jaime were looking to buy. Right now, they were crammed in her studio apartment with her two cats. Jaime truly loved her because there was no way I would've sold my house in the suburbs to downsize and live in the city.

"Don't forget to send outfit ideas for your date tonight. Just because you're married now doesn't mean we have to change our date night ritual."

"A lot has changed over the last year, but our friendship is one thing that will remain the same." With that, she hugged me tightly and we got in our cars.

Once I reached my condo, I killed the engine of my Honda Accord and headed inside. While slipping off my black suede flats, I hung my keys on the hook to the right of my front door. Like clockwork, my mother called for our weekly conversation — her mostly gossiping about the drama in our hometown.

"How was your week, Shi?" she asked after giving a rundown of her week.

"It was okay," I replied as I walked down the hall to my bedroom.

She hummed before saying, "Guess who I ran into yesterday?"

While sitting at the foot of my bed, I rolled my eyes.

Something told me she was about to mention the one person I asked her never to bring up.

"Greg."

There was a long awkward pause. I felt the heat rising in my body at the mention of his name. If only my mama knew he wasn't as perfect as he portrayed, she wouldn't be working overtime to get us back together.

"Mama." I groaned before putting the call on speaker.

"Listen, he asked for your number—"

"I know you didn't..." I growled.

He blew up my phone for months before I finally got a new number. When my number changed, he proceeded to stalk me by coming to my mama's house every night. I was forced to quit my job and move from Richmond, Virginia to Washington, D.C. Luckily, I was able to find a new job and buy a condo before having to file a restraining order.

"No, listen. I took his number and promised to pass it along. Shi, he looked *so* sad. Even after two years he still misses you."

I rolled my eyes, again. This call had to end soon before I said something disrespectful to mama. There's no way in hell I was going to call Greg. The last two years have been peaceful and stress-free why couldn't mama see how much better my life was without him?

"Mama, please stop. I'm not taking his number nor am I calling him."

"Fine! When you end up old and alone, don't come crying to me."

"I won't," I said before ending the call.

After taking a quick shower, I dressed in all black from the fedora that covered my brown shoulder length Sisterlocks, to the black knee-length boots on my feet. The fedora I wore every week provided a shield from the audience. Before moving away, I wasn't given the time or space to deal with Greg's possessiveness and my lack of self-esteem, so poetry was my way of dealing with my heartbreak. Between him damn near stalking me, and my mother constantly in my ear, it was hard for me to move on.

Ellie sent me a picture of the red dress she wore for her date and I replied with the same all-black attire I wore every week. I looked over my appearance once more time before grabbing my red leather journal that held all my poetry.

During my ride to *Ray's*, I replayed the conversation I had with my mother. It's like Greg had been watching me because every time he became an afterthought, he managed to pop up and attempt to disrupt my life. Six months ago, while I was home visiting Mama, he coincidentally stopped by her house. I know she told him I'd be in town, but to this day she still claims she had no idea he was coming by.

That was the last time I set foot in Richmond. I feel bad for going so long without seeing my mother, but until she fully came to terms with the fact that Greg and I were done, I couldn't risk my mental and emotional health by going there.

A few minutes later, I arrived at Ray's to a packed

parking lot. I was later than usual due to my conversation with my mother and I hope that didn't prevent me from signing up to perform. After parking my car, I walked to the front of the line. Since I was a regular, I had the luxury of skipping the line that snaked around the side of the building.

"Well if it isn't my favorite poet," Mel, the bouncer said, as he motioned me to walk through the door.

"Oh stop," I replied while holding my head down. My cheeks flushed at his compliment. "You think Summer will let me sign up to perform tonight? I'm a few minutes late."

Mel smiled before waving me off. "Of course she will. You're a favorite around here. She should be by the bar hurry up and catch her so she can add your name to the list."

I nodded and held my journal close to my stomach. As I walked through the lounge, I looked around at everyone. People were drinking and smoking hookah while listening to the performer on stage. The vibe at Ray's was always chill. Just like Mel said, Summer was at the bar with her clipboard in hand. She smiled as soon as our eyes connected, and she started writing.

"I just added your name!" she yelled over the sultry music. "I was beginning to think you weren't coming."

"I was running behind tonight," I yelled back.

"No worries. You're up next, after Marq."

Marq.

In the six months that he'd been performing here, he'd become a guilty pleasure of mine. There was something about his acoustic renditions of songs that ignited a fire within my soul. He had a special mystique that pulled me in like a magnet every time he entered the room.

Whenever he performed, I hung on to his every word yearning for more. His voice was so deep that I felt my soul quiver as he spoke into the mic. One night we locked eyes and instantly I was lost in his smoky gray eyes, I felt he was looking directly into my soul.

The night we locked eyes was the most interaction we had. I was too shy to approach him, and he seemed to have an unofficial fan club. Women flocked to the stage once he finished his performances taking turns fawning over him and I couldn't blame them.

He smiled and entertained them for a few before heading to the booth in the far-left corner. When I performed, I did all I could to avoid looking in his direction, but I could still feel his eyes on me.

After the current performer finished their set, I ordered my usual— a pomegranate martini and got comfortable at the bar. While Marq adjusted the mic stand, I took a gulp of my drink. Tonight, he wore a white button up covered by a leather jacket and a pair of black pants. His hair had grown out a bit since last week, but the sides were faded, and his goatee looked like it was freshly trimmed encasing his full brown lips. There was a natural glow on his copper-colored skin that couldn't be ignored. When he was ready, he looked out into the crowd and smiled.

"Good evening, everybody. How y'all feeling?" His

southern roots were evident in the drawl that escaped his lips every time he spoke. A few of the women in the audience screamed and he laughed lightly making my heart rate increase and mouth dry.

"How you feeling, baby?" a woman screamed causing the room to erupt into laughter.

A sexy smile spread across his face only making the woman in the audience scream louder. He sat on the stool and rested his guitar on his left thigh.

"I'm feeling good." His gravelly voice echoed throughout the silent lounge as all eyes were on him. I fidgeted in my seat as I unashamedly lusted over him.

"Birds flying high, you know how I feel." His fingers strummed the strings of the guitar as he hummed lowly into the mic. "*Sun in the sky you know how I feel.*"

While he performed all eyes were on him. I knew I wasn't the only one who felt his magnetic energy. By the time he finished singing, everyone was on their feet giving him a round of applause. I'm sure he would perform again before the night was over. Summer always asked people who received standing ovations to close out the night. I was already a ball of nerves and the praise he received only made my nervousness intensify. How could I follow that?

After downing the rest of my drink, I tipped the bartender and headed toward the stage. On the way there, I was greeted by other regulars who looked forward to my poems weekly. Originally, I planned on reciting a poem I wrote earlier in the week, but after my conversation with Mama, I wanted to do something I dedicated to Greg.

"Up next, we have the beautiful and tooth-achingly sweet, Shi!" Summer hugged me before walking off the stage.

"This piece is entitled *Dear Ex-Lover.*" I released a breath before looking straight ahead making sure I didn't have direct eye contact with anyone. Marq was standing to my right with his arms folded over his chest. Quickly, I looked his way before adjusting the microphone stand. I closed my eyes and allowed myself to get lost in my words.

I am sorry

I am sorry for being too great...too worthy

I am sorry for being the perfect definition of beauty and resilience that it made you feel insecure

My presence made you feel that you had to break me

I am sorry

I'm sorry that with my light it made your shadow even darker

If we walked into a room together, no one ever saw you

I'm sorry you felt intimidated

I'm sorry you thought the other women would make me feel jealous

I am sorry that they will never amount to me

I'm sorry for the nights when you lay with her and you have to fight the urge of thinking of me

Please know that I am sincerely sorry for all of your miserable days

When I finished my poem, he was still there staring at me. Heat surrounded me when our eyes connected, and he refused to look away. His lips parted as I walked down the steps and back into the crowd. Before he could say anything to me, one of his groupies grabbed his hand pulling him away. He looked back at me with a smile on his face and he winked before finally disappearing into the crowded lounge.

CHAPTER 2

"YOU SOUNDED AMAZING TONIGHT, MARQUIS," Solé purred in my ear while leaning forward giving me a better view of her cleavage spilling over the tight dress she wore.

I offered her a half-hearted smile before finishing my drink. After Shi finished her performance, Solé pulled me to the bar. That had become our thing, sitting at the bar after my performance to talk about our week. It was a routine I wanted to break, but it was easier said than done.

"What are you doing later?" Solé asked, pulling me out of my thoughts.

"I don't know yet," I answered before waving the bartender down.

For some reason, Solé's presence was aggravating me tonight. We'd been messing around for a few months, but never anything serious. She'd find me; we'd have a drink or two, and end the night end up back at my place. Come Saturday morning, she would leave without a word and the following Friday; we'd do it all over again. Our arrangement was pretty straightforward and didn't require much work. I had no problem with it because truthfully, I couldn't offer her more.

Before she could respond, Shi came over and sat to the left of me. Although Solé was damn near in my lap, I was still able to get a quick look at Shi. After placing her order, she took off the black fedora that covered her beautiful locs. She was dressed in all black with her signature red lipstick that I liked.

The longer I stared the more intrigued I was with her impenetrable demeanor. Every week, she recited her poetry and prose, then left before the night ended. She and Summer seemed close from the few interactions I'd seen them share, but other than that she stayed to herself.

"I'll be back," Solé whispered in my ear before walking away toward a small group of women who I learned were her friends. With her finally out of my hair, I was able to give Shi my undivided attention. I'd always wanted to ask her about her poetry, but the opportunity never presented itself.

"How long have you been writing?" I asked while leaning closer to her.

She hesitated before placing her hand on the red notebook beside her. "Since I was twelve."

I nodded. "That's dope. I can tell it's from the heart." A smile played at the corners of her lips before she covered it with her glass. “Marquis Kent,” I offered and held out my hand.

“Shiloh Hurston,” she returned before shaking my hand. “Where are you from?” she asked now fully facing me and giving me better access to her slanted coffee-colored eyes. They were just as rich as her brown skin.

“Lithonia, Georgia,” I said proudly.

“Your accent is thick. What made you want to move up north?”

“Needed a change.”

She nodded with a sigh like she knew exactly what I meant. There was a brief silence between us. I grabbed my drink and took a gulp. The thought of my sudden relocation was enough to shift my mood.

“Come with me,” I said as I stood from the bar stool. She looked at me skeptically before obliging my request. There was a hint of caution and curiosity in her eyes. After retrieving a twenty from my wallet, I paid the bartender for our drinks and led the way through the lounge. I motioned for her to slide into the u-shaped booth before I placed my guitar case on the side of our booth.

“How long have you been playing?” she nodded her head toward my guitar case.

“Since I was a kid. I don’t remember the exact age. I just remember always having a guitar in my hands,” I said while stroking my chin.

She smiled before saying, “You’re really talented, and your singing is breathtaking.”

The smile that appeared on my face caught me off guard. I was never one to blush, but the genuineness in her tone and the sincere look in her eyes did something to me. Memories of singing in my dad's choir came to mind and my smile grew wider, as much as I needed to leave Lithonia, I missed it and my family like crazy.

"Thank you, love."

There was a brief silence between us. Shi seemed to be wrapped up in her thoughts, while I was questioning my sudden interest in her. Six months and we've never had any interaction, not even a hello as we passed each other after performances.

"How long have you and your *ex-lover* been broken up?"

She laughed lightly before saying, "Not long enough."

I nodded, sensing her discomfort I changed the topic.

"How did you find *Ray's*?"

"What do you mean?" She narrowed her eyes slightly before licking her bottom lip.

"I know you're not from here. I would've bumped into you somewhere else by now." I leaned back and placed my arm behind her.

She leaned forward slightly and laughed. "I live in D.C. I stumbled upon Roseville while on my way back from Philadelphia. The gas station attendant told me about the Rose Festival happening at the park. I stopped for gas and the sight of all the roses intrigued me. One of the vendors was Mykel and he was also promoting open mic night at *Ray's*, so I decided to come back the following Friday. I've been coming ever since."

Mykel was an artist in every sense of the word. He did spoken word, painted, and wrote self-help books. He was one of the first people I ever met when I moved here. He often performed at *Ray's* but now that he's working on his next book, he'd been missing in action.

"You ever been to D.C.?" she asked resting her chin on her hands with a beguiling smile.

It's crazy how something as simple as her smile made my heart rate speed up. Her beautiful caramel-colored skin gleamed under the intimate lighting of the lounge. Just as I was answering her question, the intermission for open mic night ended. Summer introduced the next performer and my attention went back to Shi. She watched attentively as the group of singers assembled their instruments and microphones. From the corner of my eye, I saw Solé walking our way. Shi seemed to have noticed her too cause she chuckled.

"The president of your fan club doesn't look very happy."

"Fan club?"

"Oh, come on. Don't act like you don't know how bad *every* woman in here wants you."

"Does that include you?" I asked with a raised brow.

We stared at each other for a moment, her coffee-colored eyes alluring, yet wistful. After a few more seconds, she sighed while shaking her head before sliding out of the other side of our booth.

"It was nice talking to you, but I have to go." She

held her hand out for me to shake and my brows drew together.

"Stay until the end," I said a little too eagerly but didn't care. Grabbing her hand, I pulled her closer to me and stared up at her. "It's ending soon. Just stick around have another drink on me."

Slowly, she removed her hand from my mine. "That's why they're all over you," she said under her breath with an assessing look in her eyes. Without another word, she walked away and sat at the bar. Solé walked past Shi with a scowl on her face. When she was within an arm-length she huffed with her hands on her hips.

"Really, Marq? You're flirting with *her*."

Jealousy didn't look good on Solé and it was only adding to my already growing frustration with her possessive and clingy behavior.

"I thought you weren't the *jealous type*?" I said using her words against her. In the beginning, she was the main one pushing for us to do our own thing. She knew my situation and figured it was best we didn't put a title or any pressure to commit.

"I'm not. I'm just surprised you're interested in *her*." She folded her arms over her chest and raised her brow. The way she kept referring to Shi as her, didn't sit well with me. "She's not even your type," she stated matter-of-factly.

"You don't know my type."

She leaned down to my ear and said, "Trust me, I do." She kissed my cheek before walking away again.

I brushed off her snarky remark and scanned the room for Summer, anticipating her telling me it's time for me to get back on stage. While I waited for her, I went over to my boys Khalil and Ryder. I already knew the song I wanted to sing and needed their help. With Khalil on the drums and Ryder on the keys, it'd be executed perfectly. I met them through Summer when I first moved to Roseville. They also introduced me to their friend Taj, and from there we became *The Crew.* I told them the song I wanted to play and as luck would have it, they were familiar and agreed to join me on stage.

Across the room, I saw Summer waving her clipboard to get my attention. I nodded slightly letting her know I was on the way but not before I stopped by the bar to check on Shi. She was seated at the end of the bar with her legs crossed and a drink in her hand. When our eyes met, I winked, and she took a sip of her drink. Afterward, I headed to the stage and waited for Summer to announce the next act.

"Looks like we are in for a special treat." She looked between me, Ryder, and Khalil. "Ladies are you ready to hear how these men are going to serenade us?" There were a few screams and shrills. Summer patted me on the shoulder while she walked down the steps. Ryder held out his hand to assist her off the last step and she smiled.

"Okay, Casanova," Khalil teased.

Ryder just smiled slyly as we set up our instruments.

Once we were all set, Khalil tapped his drum sticks together three times giving us the signal to go.

"This is for you." I stepped back from the mic and looked right at Shi. The lightning in the lounge prevented me from seeing her reaction. But I'm confident that she was smiling, blushing even. The thought of her sweet smile was enough to make me smile. I stepped to the mic. *"Such a beautiful lady. The kind you find in a dream. And dreams are so real for me..."*

I looked out into the crowd at the people swaying from side to side. There were also couples slow dancing together.

Such a woman of quality

Your body's so supreme

When you dance you sway so elegantly

Girl, you simply dazzle me

A few women came to the stage and started recording us. I turned and looked at Khalil who'd taken off his t-shirt and was clearly zoned out.

I gotta stop to look

'Cause girl you look so damn good to me

So fine, lady

Thoughts of Shi's pretty brown skin and her angelic smile came to mind as I ended our performance. She was such a mystery to me, but she gave me just enough to want to know more. Her laid back demeanor was refreshing compared to Solé and the other women I'd interacted with since moving here.

After the last note played and we left the stage, I

moved as swiftly as I could through the crowd to get back to her. I was stopped a few times by people who were showing love and complimented my voice. Low key, I was interested in hearing her thoughts on my performance and just spending more time getting to know her.

But by the time I made it back to the bar, she was gone.

CHAPTER 3

I DID as he asked and stayed. But the second the open mic night ended, I rushed for the door. The conversation we had was innocent and I wanted to keep it that way. I'm sure that was a part of his game. Make a woman feel comfortable with innocent conversation, offer to buy her a drink, and then end the night in his bed together. I wasn't falling for that.

For all, I know he could have a whole family that he abandoned back in Georgia or maybe he and the president of his fan club were in a relationship. The mean side eye she was giving tonight were signs of a woman who claimed her stake on a man. All the possible scenarios of his love life played in my head as I watched him perform.

He was truly mesmerizing from his gray eyes to his southern accent. The brief conversation we had was far more fulfilling than the last few dates I'd been on combined. I sighed before sipping my martini. He looked into the crowd and winked at me...at least I think he did. It could've been for the group of ladies who were seated in front of me.

I took another sip of my drink before placing the glass back on the bar behind me. After he finished his performance, I adjusted my fedora on my head, grabbed my journal off the bar and rushed for the door. Just as I was about to rush out the door, Summer stopped me to extend the same invitation she did every week.

"Come to *8ball* with us." She smiled and grabbed my shoulder. "And don't give me no crap about having to drive home. It's only 11 o'clock. The night is still young."

Naturally, I shook my head declining her offer. Outside of her and Mel, I knew no one in Roseville and didn't feel comfortable being out until the wee hours of the morning. I liked Summer, but I wasn't sure if she was the flaky type or what she was like outside of *Ray's*.

"It'll be fun. Wings, beer, and fine men like *Marq* shooting pool and talking shit." She winked before a full smile spread across her almond-colored skin. She placed her ink pen behind her ear and raised her brows in anticipation of my response.

Heat flooded my cheeks at mentioning his name. I was hoping no one saw our interaction because I know how easily rumors can start especially in a place as small and close-knit at *Ray's*.

"I really need to head home."

"Why?" the sound of his voice made my heart beat increase.

"Yeah, why?" Summer asked, her innocent smile turning mischievous.

"Long ride back and it's pretty late," I said while turning to him. My neck was slightly craned so I could look him in the eye. Instinctively, I grabbed the top of my hat so it wouldn't fall off. His eyes bore into mine making butterflies erupt in my stomach.

"Stay an hour. If you don't enjoy yourself, we won't invite you again. Right, Summer?"

She nodded. "Right."

While I contemplated my next move, Marq kept his eyes on me almost like he was reading me.

Why was I in such a rush to get home?

I was itching to finish season one of *Russian Doll* and I know in the morning, Ellie is going to call me to tell me about her date with Jaime. Maybe if I went out, I would have a story to share too instead of gushing over her marriage.

"One hour," I said after careful consideration. He smiled again and nodded before grabbing my hand. The nighttime breeze welcomed us as we stepped outside. He continued to hold my hand as we walked toward Main Street which was adjacent to *Ray's*.

"We're walking?" I asked way more incredulously than I meant, but he didn't seem affected by my tone.

"It's a short walk, I promise. Plus, I want to drop my guitar off at my place first. Is that cool?"

I nodded and continued to follow his lead. When we arrived at *Woody's* an antique and custom furniture shop, I asked, "Why are we here?"

"My place is upstairs." My hand slid from his firm hold. "I work here and the owner, Woodrow, rents the studio to me." He motioned for me to follow him as we walked down the alley to a side door. Marq pulled out his keys and opened the door and reached for my hand again. "Be careful, this hall is dark," he instructed as he stalked up the steps.

As soon as we reached the top, I was greeted by the smell of cinnamon and nutmeg. His studio was warm and comfortable. He turned on the light and slipped off his shoes before walking over to his bed. I unzipped my boots and took them off as I continued to survey the room. Marq's place looked like something straight out of a magazine. Everything flowed together and looked nothing like any bachelor pad I'd ever seen. His furniture was all brown and ivory with hints of burnt orange throughout.

"Make yourself comfortable," he shouted from the bathroom before closing the door.

I took my fedora off and placed my journal on the small round coffee table before me. The brown suede sofa was placed in the center of the room. To my right were the stairs we climbed and to my left was his kitchen where there was a small island in the center with one barstool. Behind me was his bedroom area with a king-sized bed against the exposed brick wall. In the corner were three guitars; two acoustic and one electric – the one he played tonight. Without thinking, I walked over the guitars to get a closer look. The Mahogany-colored electric guitar had the words

Grayson inscribed on it. I ran my fingers down its smooth finish.

"You like it?" Marq asked making me jump.

With a quick nod, I answered his question before walking toward the couch to sit. I watched Marq change out of his button up to a black t-shirt that fit just right showing off his muscular arms. My intrusive behavior didn't go unnoticed as Marq winked before pulling the shirt down to cover his six-pack. After putting his jacket on, he walked over to me with a sly smirk on his face.

"Ready?"

"Yup." I reached for my hat and he grabbed my hand stopping me.

"You don't need that. On the way back to your car we'll come to get your things."

I swallowed down the lump in my throat. Between this pensive look in his eyes and the feel of his hand on mine yet again, heat was coursing through my veins at record speed. He dropped my hand and grabbed a small bag off the island before reaching for my hand again leading us back down the steps.

During our short walk to *8Ball*, he asked how I felt about his performance. I was honest in telling him I enjoyed it and tried to stop my heart from beating out of my chest when he admitted that it was dedicated to me.

8Ball looked just as I imagined a pool hall to be. It was dark with lights hanging over the four pool tables placed directly in the center of the room. The bar was crowded with people from the open mic night and a few motorcyclists.

Marq quickly scanned the room before he found Summer, Mel, and a few other people I'd only seen in passing. Summer came to me and threw her arm around my shoulder.

"Thanks for coming. I get tired of being the only woman with these clowns," she said while smiling at the group of men. "This is Taj, Ryder, and Khalil." She introduced me to the men who often performed as a group and sometimes individually.

"I just ordered another round," Mel said before he sat down at the table, they'd made ours for the night. "Hey, Shi." He winked before turning his attention to the TVs above the bar.

"Hey, Marq, did you bring the quarters?" Summer asked before sitting next to Mel.

"Right here," he said holding up the bag. When Marq saw the confused expression on my face he went on to explain. "We take turns bringing money for the jukebox." He pointed at the machine by motioning his head to the left. "Come pick out some songs with me."

After taking off my jacket and placing on the seat I'd deemed mine, I followed Marq over to the jukebox. He put in three dollars' worth of quarters before he stepped to the side. "Pick three songs."

While chewing on my bottom lip, I sifted through the extensive catalog of music. After a few moments, I made a selection. Marq laughed when I selected *7/11* by Beyoncé.

God, his laugh was heavenly.

"What?" I asked out of curiosity.

"I knew you'd pick a Beyoncé song. You have *Beyhive* written all over you."

With a light laugh, I asked, "What do you mean?"

"Dressed in all black and the fedora gives *Formation* vibes," he said easily before leaning against the wall.

"Guilty."

He smiled again and his smoky-gray eyes darkened. "So, why do you wear a fedora every time you're at *Ray's*?"

I continued to look through the music as I thought over his question.

"It makes me feel…" I paused not really sure if I wanted to be honest with him or not.

"Invisible?" he guessed. My eyes shot to his and I nodded. "You shouldn't want to be invisible. You're too damn beautiful to be hiding behind a big ass hat."

I pulled my bottom lip between my teeth to hide my growing smile, but I knew he saw it because he smiled too. He stared at me for a minute before coming and standing behind me with his hands resting on both sides of the jukebox caging me in. Like his studio, he smelled like cinnamon and nutmeg. He made himself comfortable by resting his chin on my shoulder. The warm sensation that overcame me was foreign, but I wasn't complaining. After selecting two more songs, we returned to the group and took our seats at the table.

The nervousness I felt about coming out with them slowly dissipated as I engaged in conversation with this interesting group of people. After a few shots, I loosened up. I shared with them a little about my poetry and where I got my inspiration to write. The guys shared how they learned to play their instruments. Everyone was born and raised in Roseville except Marq and Ryder – who moved here a year ago after a divorce.

Eventually, the guys went to play pool, leaving Summer and me to get to know each other better. Summer works as a hair stylist during the week and hosts events part-time mostly at *Ray's.* I always suspected she was into cosmetology. Every month her hair was a different color or style. This month she's rocking a platinum-blonde fade with a side part. She also shared what each of the guys did. Mel worked as a security guard at the bank located near city hall and on the weekends worked at *Ray's*. Taj and Ryder worked as mechanics at the only body shop in town, while Khalil wrote for the *Roseville Gazette,* the town's only newspaper.

The guys had been playing pool for the last hour while Summer and I played Pac Man. It was close to one when I realized my hour had come and gone. It was safe to say; I was truly enjoying myself.

"Wanna play a game with me?" Marq asked with two pool sticks in hand.

"I don't know how to play," I admitted, before sipping a glass of water the waitress just brought to me.

"I'll teach you." His voice dropped an octave and made my center tighten. He handed me the shorter of the two sticks and walked to the table closest to us. He placed the balls in the triangle thing then pulled me to the front end of the table. "You're going to break."

I stared at him blankly.

Obviously, he didn't understand that I knew nothing about playing pool. I grabbed the chalk and ran it over the tip of my stick before trying my best to hit the center ball. The cue ball went to the left of the table and slowed. Marq's laughter made me laugh although I was slightly annoyed.

"Come here," he said while motioning his hand. "Stand here." He grabbed my waist and positioned me in front of the head spot, as he called it. "I'm going to teach you how to do a closed bridge."

He placed my hand flat on the table, then he laid the stick across my thumb knuckle, and across the knuckle of my middle finger. He told me to curl your index finger around the shaft of the stick and spread my fingers. After he taught me how to do a closed bridge, he positioned my elbow so that it was vertical aligning with my back.

When he leaned over me and helped me align the stick perfectly with the cue ball, I took an opportunity to take in his warm scent. The simple act of him teaching how to play pool shouldn't have turned me on as much as it did.

"Ready?" he asked, his voice low and enticing.

With my tongue pressed to the corner of my mouth, I nodded and pulled my arm back before striking the cue ball. My eyes widened as I watched the cue ball break numbered balls and they scattered across the table.

Unfortunately, none of them fell into a pocket, but the fact that I actually hit a ball was enough for me.

I turned to Marq with a wide smile that he returned before saying, "I hope you enjoy this ass whooping as much as I enjoy giving it to you."

"Challenge accepted," I said with a nod.

After three games, I gave up. Marq held no remorse as he showed off his pool playing skills, even teaching me a thing or two. The way he bit his bottom lip and closed his right eye while preparing for the next shot was drool-worthy. Every time he made a ball go into the pocket, he'd look at me and wink, before showcasing his perfect smile. He knew I was focusing more on *him* than I was our game, which is part of the reason why I lost.

If this was the first date, I would go down as one of my favorites. Our chemistry was mystifying, and flirting came naturally. And it wasn't always verbal. It was the subtle looks, the way he'd walk behind me and gently place his hand on my waist.

I even found myself putting a little extra arch in my back when preparing to shoot. The lustful look in his eyes let me know I was succeeding in the flirtatious game we were playing. As the crowded bar started to empty, *The Crew,* as the called themselves, all said their goodbyes and planned for next week's meet up.

"I'm so glad you came out. Hopefully, you'll join us again?" Summer asked while hugging me. I nodded before handing her my phone to enter her number.

Everyone went their separate ways, while Marq and I headed back to his place.

“Hungry?” he asked. “I know a great diner not too far from here.”

“Lead the way,” I said with a smile.

The thought of spending more one on one time with him made me giddy inside, a feeling that was foreign to me. I wasn't sure where this night would lead us, but I was thoroughly enjoying every second of the spontaneity.

CHAPTER 4

"DO you always walk the streets of Roseville at this hour?" she asked as we neared the *Over Easy Diner*.

"Yes, believe it or not." My response shocked her as she stopped in her tracks.

"Why?"

After opening the door for her, I said, "I'm a night owl."

The look on her face told me she wanted to know more but decided to drop the subject which I was happy with because that could take us down a road I'm not willing to confront yet.

We walked to my designated booth in the far left corner. Shi took her seat then looked around the nearly empty diner. Roseville was a ghost town at this hour. The only people who came to this diner on Friday nights were me, truck drivers, and people who stumbled upon this town while on a road trip.

Mirian, the owner of *Over Easy* had become my

surrogate mother away from home. She expected me every morning for breakfast, except on Saturdays because she knew I'd be coming in the wee hours after open mic night on Friday's

"Well, hello there," Mirian said as she grabbed her notepad from her apron pocket.

"Hey, Mimi," I replied with a smile.

Shi looked back and forth at Mirian and me with a confused expression on her pretty little face.

"This is the owner of the diner, Mirian. Mirian this is my new friend, Shiloh."

"New friend, huh?" Mirian smiled and raised her brow. "He usually comes here alone; I was starting to get worried. Been here for a little over six months and hadn't made one friend aside from me of course." Shi smiled and leaned back in her seat.

"I have friends," I said after laughing.

Mirian hummed before writing down my order on her notepad. There was no need for her to ask, since my first visit, my order had remained consistent — two eggs over easy, turkey bacon, toast, grits, and a glass of water.

"Do you need time to look over the menu, sweetie?" Mirian asked Shi.

She nodded before grabbing a menu from behind the mini jukebox on our table. Mirian tucked her notepad away before walking toward her son who was also the chef.

"You're so friendly," Shi said while looking over the menu.

I shrugged before saying, "Where I'm from this is normal behavior. Plus, you never know who you'll need in the future." I leaned forward and pressed my elbows on the table. "When I first moved here, I was staying at the motel right off the exit." Shi scrunched her nose and I nodded. "Yeah, same reaction my sister had. Anyway, we came here for dinner and Mirian being Mirian, she questioned our visit. I told her I was here for a fresh start, needed a job, and a place to live. She and Woodrow are good friends, so she put me on. I had a job within 24 hours. Imagine if I would've been rude or short when she introduced herself. I'd prolly still be at that roach motel."

Shi nodded and drummed her fingers on the table. "So, you have a sister?"

"Yes, Monica. She's two years older than me at 30. What about you?"

She shifted in her seat before shaking her head. "Only child."

"So, you're spoiled?" I teased. I was relieved when she laughed instead of being offended by my joke. She had a sense of humor, another thing that I found extremely attractive about her.

"Just a little."

Mirian returned to our table with our waters. "Ready, sweetie?" she asked Shi.

"I'll take the southwestern omelet and a side of grits please."

"You got it."

Once Mirian left, a comfortable silence fell over us.

I took my time looking over her features. Now that she wasn't *hiding* behind those hats, I could get a good look at her. Shiloh was nothing short of beautiful. Her dark brown skin was flawless and had a natural glow that made me wonder why she was so eager to hide it. When my eyes connected with hers, she diverted her attention to the jukebox. I reached in my pocket and handed her the remaining quarters I had left over from *8Ball*. She selected *The Beautiful Ones* by Prince and we both nodded our heads to the sounds of Prince and the Revolution.

"Tell me about you," I said, breaking the silence.

"What do you want to know?" she asked while running her fingers through her hair. Her locs that she pushed back, fell to the side framing her face. While staring at her pensively, I took a minute to think. What did I want to know about the mysterious woman in front of me?

"What made you perform '*Dear Ex-Lover'* tonight?" Her eyes widened then lowered as she sighed. "Typically, your performances align with your mood. Like last month, you talked about freedom and what it meant to you. You said something '*I'm like free as the birds in the sky and calm as the ocean waters crashing against the shore.*' You looked at peace when you performed it too. But tonight, you looked every bit of pissed."

"Wow," was all she said.

"Was that too much?" I asked sensing a shift in her mood.

She shook her head. “You’re *very* observant.”

“Only when it’s something that catches my eye.”

She laughed quietly then shook her head. Before I could ask what was on her mind, Mirian came over with our food.

“Let me know if y’all need anything.” I nodded and Mirian went to greet her next table.

Seeing Shi light up at the sight of her food made me smile. Truthfully, I wanted to see more of this side of her.

“You didn't answer my question,” I said before taking a bite of my toast.

“My mother pissed me off.”

I quirked my brow. “So, you did a poem dedicated to your ex?”

“She ran into him recently and he asked for my number.” After running her fingers through her hair, she continued, “My mom wants me to get back with him, marry him, have his children, and… I just can’t.”

“You still love him?”

She shook her head fleetingly. “Not at all. He’s a man that’s used to getting what he wants, and I just wish he would give me the space I deserve.”

There was a slight pause, I sensed her hesitation when it came to opening up about her ex. I didn't want to seem pushy or nosy so, I changed the subject.

“You from D.C?”

“Nope, Richmond.”

“What made you leave?”

She sighed. “Him.”

Damn.

She slid the remaining quarters across the table and inserted them into the jukebox. While she looked through the music selections, I continued to eat my food while occasionally stealing glances at her. I tried not to look like a creep, but I couldn't help myself. Tonight feels like the first time I *saw* Shiloh. The sounds of Etta James' *I'd Rather Go Blind* came on and she returned attention to me.

"So, what's up with you and *the president* of your unofficial fan club?" she asked with a playful smile.

"Nothing is up between us."

She raised her brow and twisted her lips like she wasn't convinced.

"We have an arrangement. When we're together, we're together. And we're not together…" I shrugged while taking a bite of my bacon.

"You look like the type to have commitment issues."

I shook my head. If only she knew that was far from my case. Having a family and a wife was something I hoped to have in the future, but right now I was focused on getting back on my feet. Moving from the only place I'd ever called home was a big step and living on my own was needed right now. Over the last few years, I depended heavily on my Pops and sister and now that I was on the cusp of thirty it was time for me to get my shit together.

"Nah, that's far from the truth."

"So, what *is* the truth?" she pried.

"I want a wife, two kids, a house with a white picket fence."

She giggled, then said, "For real?"

"Why is that so hard to believe?"

"I don't know...because you seem kind of like a ho."

I laughed at her brutal honesty. If I were her, I could see why she thought I was a ho. Women literally clung to me at Ray's and while I didn't exactly give them the attention they desperately fought for, I wasn't turning them away either. It may seem egotistical, but I liked the attention. Although, I'd prefer if the attention I received was from someone I wanted to reciprocate, like Shiloh.

"So does your ex have you all messed up about future relationships?"

"Messed up? No. It wasn't all him. I had to accept my part in all the foolishness that transpired between us."

I nodded before asking, "What's your ideal kind of partner?"

She looked out the window then back at me. "Trustworthy, dependable, and hopelessly devoted to me." Sadness lingered in her eyes for a beat then she smiled. "I want a Sunday kind of love."

I raised my brow and her smile grew wider as she laughed.

"You know? Like the song." She pointed her head toward the jukebox. "Easy, refreshing, and carefree."

She stared at me for a few moments with a thoughtful expression before gazing out the window.

When she looked back at me, the once thoughtful look was replaced with one I couldn't read.

"It's getting pretty late," she said finally.

I pulled out a twenty-dollar bill and dropped in on the table before reaching for her hand. Mirian waved from her seat behind the counter and we waved back before starting our walk back to *Ray's*. Her car was the only car left in the parking lot. After she unlocked the doors, I opened hers before going to the passenger's side. The drive to my place was quick. Just as she parked the car, she let out a long yawn.

"You wanna crash at my place?" I asked concerned for her safety. D.C was a good thirty-minute drive, but the roads were dark, and we were known to have a few accidents due to deer crossing the road. She eyed me suspiciously. "I'll sleep on the couch. I don't bite." I held up my hands in surrender.

As she thought over my offer, she chewed on her bottom lip and drummed her thumbs against her steering wheel. "Okay. But I'm leaving first thing in the morning and don't try anything."

"Cool," I said before opening the passenger door.

Once we were inside, I went to my closet and grabbed a new pack of t-shirts then tossed it to her. Working as a carpenter had me running through t-shirts more than I liked. It didn't help that I liked to wear them outside of working as well. While she changed in my bathroom, I went to my closet and changed into a pair of sweats. It was a little after three in the morning and I was nowhere near sleepy. Maybe once Shiloh fell asleep, I would sit on my balcony and play around with my guitar.

The sound of her clearing her throat pulled me out of my thoughts. She stood in the door frame of my closet with her clothes folded neatly in her arms. My t-shirt stopped mid-thigh on her petite frame. My eyes had a mind of their own as they slowly trailed her body from her pink colored toes to her face. She was biting on her bottom lip with flushed cheeks when we made eye contact.

"Thanks for the shirt," she said in a quiet, yet sweet whisper.

"No problem, love."

I grabbed a set of fresh sheets from the top shelf before hitting the switch and walking over to my bed. Shiloh followed close behind while still holding onto her belongings firmly.

"Put your stuff over there." I pointed to the bar stool at my kitchen island.

"Let me help you," she offered after putting her stuff down. Without direction, she pulled the sheets off the bed and sat them on the ottoman. I handed her the pillowcases as I put the fitted sheet on my queen-sized bed, followed by the top sheet, then finally the comforter.

"You need anything else?" I asked before grabbing one of my guitars.

"No, I'm fine."

I nodded and said, "Cool."

She settled into bed and I looked at her one last time

before I pushed the sliding door to the right and stepped onto the small balcony. There wasn't much space for more than two people. After sitting on the cheap folding chair, I started to play India Arie's *Brown Skin*. The song came to mind after seeing Shiloh standing in my closet.

My fingers were itching to touch her, but I couldn't go there with her, not after the night we had. It'd been a long time since I just kicked with a woman, even if I was attracted to her. I knew nothing would come of our little adventure tonight. Tomorrow, she'd go back home, and we would go back to seeing each other in passing. The sound of the door sliding open broke me out of my jam session and my thoughts.

"Am I too loud?" I asked as she closed the door and leaned against it. She shook her head. As I turned to face her, I noticed the sadness in her eyes. "You okay?" I placed my guitar on the chair after standing up.

"My mother gave him my damn number," she mumbled before running her hands through her hair. "I didn't answer so he left a message. Two whole minutes of him telling me how much he misses me and what we had."

I grabbed her hand. "Let's go back inside."

She sat on the couch with her legs folded. "He was married. I mean, he *is* married," she said after a long silence. "I knew he was married from day one, but I didn't care because *I* took care of him. Everything *she* didn't do, *I* did."

She paused and looked at me. Almost as if she was

waiting for me to pass some type of judgment against her, but I was in no position to do that. When she realized I had nothing to say, she continued, "It wasn't until I came face to face with his wife that I realized, I was the one getting the short end of the stick. No matter how much I filled every void she left, I could never be her. I would never have all of him."

Her shoulders slouched as she sighed. I grabbed her hand and ran my thumb across it gently. Her lips curved into a lazy smile. "You probably think I'm a shitty person, huh?"

I shook my head. "Nah, I'm no angel either."

"What's your skeleton? Can't be as bad as mine." Her grip on my hand tightened and it made me feel less insecure about my past.

"I moved here because I needed a fresh start." I sighed. "I grew up in the church. My grandfather was a pastor and my Pops followed in his footsteps, so naturally, everyone expected me to do the same. When I was about 15, my mother passed away from cancer and I was angry. The person I loved most was taken from me and I didn't know how to handle it. Losing her made angry with God and the world."

I paused and looked at Shi. Her eyes were glossy and full of questions.

"I got tired of being the *church boy* and got caught up in the streets. The crew I hung with stole cars, broke them down, then sold the parts. The first time I got caught, the judge gave me a slap on the wrist because I was *the preacher's kid*. That only made me feel more invincible. I started getting careless with the cars I stole and eventually, I got caught and was sentenced to three years. When I got out my sister and dad smothered me. My Pops understood why I was acting out and stopped putting so much pressure on me to follow in his footsteps."

Shi's mouth fell agape as she took my hands into hers. "Wow."

"Yeah," I said after releasing a breath.

"Thank you for sharing that with me."

She continued to stare at me her gaze intense and thoughtful. Whatever was on her mind she was hesitant about sharing. I wasn't going to push her, after all, I did just share something pretty heavy with her. Something only a handful of people in Roseville knew.

"Does...anyone else know?" she asked.

I nodded. "The crew knows...and Solé." She inhaled and released a slow breath. I saw the disappointment on her face, but she recovered with ease. "I told her because I thought maybe we would be more than we are. And I wanted to be as honest as possible from the jump."

"But?"

"But we will never be more. We don't have a connection outside of sex."

Her grip on my hands loosened and I felt her retreating. I'm sure unpleasant memories from her last relationship came to mind. The energy between us shifted and I knew she felt it too because her eyes told me all I needed to know. Telling her I was nothing like her ex wouldn't mean anything, I'm sure she'd been sold many dreams in the past. My actions would show her I'm different.

I pulled her onto my lap while wrapping my arms around her waist. She refused to make eye contact with me opting to give the hem of my shirt her attention while she fiddled with it. My gaze moved from her pretty brown thighs to her lips. They were so full and pink. And the longer she dug her teeth into her bottom lip, the more I wanted to taste them.

No longer able to resist, I grabbed her chin. I kissed her slowly and deliberately. I took my time tasting and savoring the feel of her soft lips against mine. She returned the pecks before allowing me to explore her fully, I slipped my tongue into her mouth and our tongues engaged in a slow dance.

She whimpered and I ran my hands under her shirt. Goosebumps covered her warm skin as my finger trailed up her rib cage and around her waist. I pulled her onto my lap and her heat covered me. My hands had a mind of their own as they took their time rubbing all over her back and eventually to the nape of her neck. I used my hand to angle her head back before kissing her neck and chin.

It was animalistic the way I was kissing her, but I didn't care. All night, I had to fight the urge to touch her beautiful brown skin, so now I held nothing back. The way her nails dug into my arms confirmed that she's been holding back too. The tension between us was boiling over. My lips returned to hers, and she bit my bottom lip before sucking it while rocking her hips against me.

A sense of urgency overcame us as I pulled her shirt over her head and pulled her closer. My hands gripped her thighs making her wrap them around me fully. I raised up and carried her over to my bed. Her lips never moved from mine as we found a rhythm of our own. She took her time exploring my lips with nips and licks while moaning a sweet tune I could listen to forever.

"Shiloh..." I pulled back and looked at her.

With her eyes still closed she half-moaned, "Yes?"

"You sure about this?"

"Yes," she answered breathlessly, her eyes opened and bored into mine. "Yes, I'm sure."

We smiled at each other before I went to my bathroom to grab protection. When I returned, she was laying on her side completely naked. She rested her cheek in her palm and her locs framed her face perfectly.

She lay on her back once I made my way over to her. While laying over her, I looked at her intently etching the sight of her silky brown skin and beautiful face into my memory.

"You're so damn beautiful," I leaned down and whispered in her ear. Her hands gripped my arms as I slid into her slippery folds. I hissed as she engulfed me with her warmth. Her nails dug deeper into my arms the further I entered her. The dim lighting from the living area allowed me to get a look at her.

"Look at me," I said with a groan.

Her eyes were low, but she never broke eye contact with me. She wrapped her legs around my waist and pushed me further into her. The sounds of pleasure escaping her lips were better than any chord I could play or note I could sing.

It wasn't long before her moans and whimpers grew louder and into her calling out my name. I felt myself becoming weaker with every thrust. She moved her pelvis to meet my thrusts and we both became unhinged. Her nails dug deeper into my arms as I buried myself inside her. I nuzzled my face in her neck as we both reached our peaks.

I fell down beside her and pulled her close to me. In no time, I heard her soft snores as she completely relaxed in my arms. There was no way we could go back to being strangers after this. I had to have more of her and not just sexually. My hold on her tightened as I finally let sleep overcome me.

The sun from my open blinds shone through and woke me from my sleep. A part of me felt like last night was a dream, like everything after *Ray's* was a figment of my imagination. When I turned over and reached for Shi, and she wasn't there I thought maybe it was all a dream. I sat up and looked around hoping maybe she was in the bathroom or maybe on my balcony.

I threw on a pair of shorts and a shirt and rushed down the stairs. The dewy morning air met me as I ran to the front of Woody's to see her car wasn't there.

She was gone.

CHAPTER 5

One week later...

I WASN'T THAT GIRL.

The girl who met a man, bared her soul to him, then slept with him all in one night. But that's exactly what I did last Friday with Marquis. And I loved every second of it. Marquis was attentive, reassuring, and just everything I wasn't expecting from *him.* When I woke up still in his arms, it scared the hell out of me. Not only was I too afraid to face him, but I was also afraid of what he thought about everything that transpired between us.

So, I left.

A whole week later, and I still wasn't ready to face him. After I told Ellie everything that went down, she chastised me for ruining a potential relationship. What else did I expect her to do? From the outside looking in, we had the perfect night from beginning to end. But neither he nor I were ready for a relationship. I had a married ex who was still trying to creep back into my life, and Marquis had a sex buddy and wasn't afraid to admit it.

The way he didn't judge me when I inadvertently admitted how I was the poster child for a woman with *daddy issues*. While I didn't share all the embarrassing details of the relationship I had with Greg – like the other women who he had no problem throwing in my face when I did get the strength to leave his trifling ass.

Greg was twenty years my senior and toward the end of our tumultuous relationship, I found out about his son who was only a year younger than me. His wife made sure to let me and everyone at my job know when she confronted me. I shuddered as the memories filled my mind.

The thought of sharing *everything* with Marq did cross my mind plenty of times that night, but what would've been the point. Yet that didn't stop me from spending each day thinking about him and the night we shared from the pool hall to his bed.

The way he constantly stayed on my mind let me know a conversation was needed, but I couldn't just say sorry. And truthfully, I didn't know where to start with apologizing for ghosting him. When the words finally did present themselves, they came in the form of a poem. My only hope was that he would be at Ray's tonight and be willing to accept my form of an apology.

I spent most of my shift staring at the clock. Time

was flying by today only adding to my anxiety about possibly seeing him tonight. At first, I wasn't going to go, but after letting Ellie read the poem, she convinced me to go. The one night when I was fully open to her coming, of course, she and Jaime were going away on a mini vacation to the mountains.

"Shi, you got this," Ellie said while patting me on the back. We were standing at our cars about to go our separate ways.

"I don't know, El." I shrugged. "I never ghosted anyone before, but I know how it feels. If I were him, I wouldn't forgive me, at least not so easily."

She smiled. "Luckily, he isn't you. From what you told me about him, he seems sweet. Just go there with an open mind."

"I'll try."

We hugged one last time before leaving.

On the way home, Mama called. Lord knows I didn't want to answer, but our weekly calls meant a lot to me and since I wasn't going home to visit any time soon, I had to talk to her as often as possible.

"I still can't believe you changed your number and didn't tell me right away!"

After Greg's call Friday night, I knew that wasn't the last time I would hear from him. To prevent any unnecessary stress, I went ahead and changed my number first thing on Monday morning. I was pissed Mama gave him my number, so I didn't immediately tell her about my new number.

"Mama, I can't believe you disregarded my wishes."

She huffed. "I'm trying to do what is best. He divorced his wife, Shiloh."

"You knew he was married?"

"Our run-in last week wasn't as quick as I made it seem. He told me everything."

Everything.

Did that include his son?

Did it include all the lies he told me about his "failing" marriage? I didn't fully believe he got a divorce from his wife nor did I care. Greg was the type to say anything to get his way.

I sighed as I pulled into my driveway. After putting the car in park, I asked, "And you still thought it was okay to give him my number?"

"People can change."

"Yeah, okay." I bit my bottom lip to prevent myself from saying more.

The tension between Mama and I was thick. We've had our fair share of disagreements when it came to the men I dated. She'd always been super opinionated when it came to my relationships. No man was ever good enough, except the *married* one. Which I found ironic because I was the product of a long-term affair.

Why would my mother want me to endure the same pain she did for years? My father came and went as he pleased; we weren't his main priority. His wife and children were, and he made it very clear when he stopped coming around. We had the '*you're the reason I have daddy issues*' argument too many times to count and if we kept at it today, would most definitely lead to another one.

After a long pause, Mama said, "But if you say you're done, then I guess I have to respect it."

"Thank you, Mama. I'll talk to you later."

I turned off my car, before unbuckling my seatbelt. For a moment, I just sat in complete silence. Once the call ended, I finally felt like that was the last time my mother would bring up Greg. Now, my mind was back on confronting Marq.

I wasted no time showering and getting dressed. Tonight, I decided on a long-sleeved black knee-length bodycon dress and a pair of black booties. My hair was in a neat bun and I decided to nix the fedora for the night. Marq's comment about me hiding behind a hat replayed and I smiled. For the first time in years, I didn't feel the need to be invisible. After applying my makeup, I was ready to go.

The parking lot at Ray's was packed and the line at the door was exceptionally long. I walked right to the front and Mel was at the door sitting on his stool.

"Well if it isn't my favorite poet," he said with a smile.

"Hey, Mel." I wrapped my arms around his neck hugging him.

"You know Summer is waiting for you. You better hurry inside."

I walked through the lounge looking for Summer

and Marq. First, I looked at the bar for him, but he wasn't there then, I looked toward the booth where we sat last week and no luck. I found Summer standing behind the bar talking to the bartender.

While I waited for their conversation to end, I scanned the crowd still in search of Marq. My stomach was in knots thinking about the words I'd written down in hopes he'd forgive me for being flaky. The longer I looked around the sadder I became at the realization that he may not be here tonight.

"Hey, girly. You look *extra* sexy tonight. I like!" Summer's voice broke me out of my thoughts. "I put you down there are two people are ahead of you."

I nodded. "Have you seen Marq?"

Summer and I texted all week and she was ready for us to have another night out. And truthfully, I was too, but that was dependent upon how open mic night went. Of course, she asked about Marq and I. I was open about my night with Marq. She didn't seem surprised when I told her how it ended. Apparently, we weren't the only ones who felt the chemistry between us was undeniable.

She frowned. "No, I haven't. He usually comes early too, but don't worry, I'm sure he'll show up." she checked the time on her watch before looking at the stage. "I'll be back."

The bartender came over with my martini and smiled. I expressed my gratitude before taking a sip. While I watched the singer on stage singing her rendition of *Come Through and Chill,* I texted Ellie giving her an update on how our plan may be a failure.

Ellie: If all else fails, go to his place.

Shi: That's some stalker mess.

Ellie: No, it's not!

I laughed before putting my phone away and returning my attention to the stage. Summer waved her hand letting me know I was next up. As I walked onto the stage, I noticed the stares and whistles I got from men and women as they admired my appearance for the night.

"Ladies and gentlemen, up next we have the incomparable Shi!" the crowd was a mixture of snapping and applause as I walked up the steps to the mic. Summer hugged me before leaving the stage.

I adjusted the mic stand and took in a deep breath. Everything looked different without the protection of my hat. I could see the faces of the people sitting in front of me. To my right, was Summer hugging her clipboard with a look of admiration.

When she smiled and gave me a thumbs up, I laughed then returned my attention back to the audience. My heart was pounding against my chest and the words I'd rehearsed in the shower wouldn't come out. So, I decided to speak from my heart.

"You ever met someone and the connection was inexplicable? It feels almost too good to be true? They make you question everyone before them and even question yourself? Well, it happened to me recently and they made me do a lot of self-reflection. They even made me think about the possibility of falling in love again." I looked out into the crowd still secretly searching for him. "I'm sorry. I'm a little nervous."

A man from the crowd shouted, "You got it, baby," and smiled.

"This poem has no title, but it was written for someone special. I hope he's here tonight." I sighed before looking down into my notebook.

Before we became intimate

I laid all of my demons in your bed

I expected you to run

I prepared myself for your departure

The next morning I woke up to you holding me tight

You decided to give a fair chance to a broken woman

20 years of my life had gone by

I never respected a man more than I did you

The crowd erupted into snaps and praises. I bit my bottom lip to hide my smile before doing a quick curtsy. As I walked off the stage, I sighed in relief. On my way to the bar, I ran into Khalil and Ryder who hugged me. Just as I was about to approach the bar my eyes landed on Marq. His back was facing me and when I finally was able, I pried my eyes away from him to see he was with her. She was practically in his lap while he talked to her.

The anger and disappointment I felt were hard to contain. A part of me wanted to go over to him, but the other part reminded me that this was all my doing. I'm the one who left like a thief in the night without a word.

I swallowed the lump in my throat before making the split decision to leave.

There was someone performing a slow song, so the floor was crowded with couples slow dancing. As I weaved in and out of the crowd, I felt my chest tightening. I couldn't get out of here fast enough. Summer grabbed my arm before and spun me around.

"Shi, wait!"

I shook my head. "I have to go, Summer."

"Before you do, I just wanted to say, you did really good tonight. I've watched you for the last two years and tonight is the most confident you've ever looked and sounded." She hugged me before I could respond, and I returned the gesture with a smile. When she released me from a much-needed embrace, she looked toward the bar where Marq was no longer sitting. "He'll come around. Don't worry."

I gave her a half-hearted smile before heading toward the door. The cool spring air welcomed me as I stepped onto the sidewalk. With my notebook pressed tightly at my side, I strode to my car. While I wish things between me and Marq could've ended differently, I can only use our encounter as a lesson of what not to do the next time I meet someone. I regret not having the chance to talk to him one-on-one, but I put myself in the position of having to see him with another woman.

"Shiloh!" his voice bellowed out into the night. I stopped for a moment, then continued to my car. His footsteps grew louder the closer he got to me. When I reached my car, I turned to face him. He pressed both hands against my car caging me in. “That’s *twice* now that you’ve dipped on me.”

His brows drew together as he scowled. The eyes that I once found to be alluring and irresistible were now dark and pensive. They set my insides ablaze and I could no longer stand looking at him, so I looked down.

“Nah, don't get all timid now. Did I do something wrong?” While shaking my head, I looked him in the eyes. “Okay, so why did I wake up alone Saturday morning?”

“I got scared,” I admitted.

He sighed. “Scared of what?”

“Scared of what comes next.” I pointed toward *Ray’s*. “Then I see you with Solé and I don’t know about this, Marquis.”

“You didn’t give us a chance to decide what comes next.” He took a step back and ran his hand over his face. My heart dropped for a second. Was this really going to be the end for us? All because I was too much of a coward to face him the morning after?

“Marq, I’m sorry for leaving.”

He looked at me only for a moment before looking past me. With his hands in his pockets, he took another step away from me. I felt another twinge of guilt in my stomach. He was slipping away from me and I wasn’t ready for this to end.

“Marq.” I tugged at the hem of his t-shirt. The silence between us was suffocating. Desperately, I needed for him to say something...anything.

“Look, you don’t need to worry about her. What you

saw back there was me ending our situation." His gaze returned to mine and his eyes softened. "'Cause who I want is right in front of me."

"I want you too."

"We don't have to figure everything out right now. Let's just enjoy each other. I promise I won't give you any reason to doubt or lose faith in me, but you have to promise the same."

My voice failed when I tried to speak, so I nodded making sure our eye contact never broke. He cupped my cheek and I exhaled. His touch was needed and thoroughly missed. While wrapping my arms around his waist, I fell back onto my car.

His full brown lips were hovering over mine inviting vivid memories of the pleasure they ensued last week. Memories of the way he trailed kisses down my neck sent chills up my spine.

If I allowed him to continue to tease me, I would've spontaneously combusted in his arms. I tilted my head just enough for our lips to touch. His mouth covered mine hungrily and I accepted all of him. Our lips molded perfectly together as we both lost ourselves in each other's embrace. Being in his arms felt safe. Something I hadn't felt from a man in a long time.

He pulled back and looked me into my eyes. Those hypnotic smoky-gray eyes made me weaker the longer I looked into them. The muscles in his jaw clenched and his Adam's apple raised and lowered.

"Your poem," he finally said.

"Yes?"

"I loved it."

He smiled and stared at me for a second longer before kissing me again. The look of adoration in his eyes made my heart melt. I melted in his arms. In the middle of the parking lot, we kissed like two love sprung teenagers and I loved every second.

CHAPTER 6

THIS WAS how I wanted to spend my Saturday's, music playing softly in the background while Shi fed me pancakes with nothing but my t-shirt on. Last night, after we talked, we went back to my place and had a replay of last week. Except for this time, it was more passion, less reservation and lasted until the sun rose. It was a little after noon when we both decided it was time to get out of bed.

Normally, I would've gone to grab something from *Over Easy,* but the thought of having to leave the comfort of my home didn't seem too exciting. Plus, I wanted to have Shi to myself for as long as possible. While she talked to her friend on my balcony, I made us breakfast. The only thing I was good at making was pancakes and eggs, thanks to my mother. Before she passed away, it was one of the few meals she taught me to make. 'Til this day, I don't know anyone who makes pancakes as fluffy and golden as her.

"These are the best pancakes I've ever had," Shiloh said in between bites.

"Thanks, love."

She smiled before sticking another fork full of pancakes in my mouth. We were seated comfortably on my floor with our plates on my coffee table. For some reason, we both loved the floor more than the couch or my bed. Since we spent most of our night there. I reached around her and grabbed my glass of orange juice and took a sip. She put the now empty plate on the table and straddled my lap. The smile on her face had been present since last night.

"I like you a lot," she blurted out before biting her bottom lip.

"I like you a lot, too."

She needed to be affirmed as much as possible. That wasn't a sign of insecurity in my eyes. I needed to feel affection which is why I held and kissed her randomly throughout the night. And why she was currently in my lap.

"I haven't been in a relationship for a long time." She sighed, and her arm loosened from around my neck.

"Neither have I. Which is why we are going to do things at our own pace."

The smile on her face was confirmation that like me she was willing to give this a try. For a minute, we just stared into each other's eyes as her fingers strummed through my hair. I ran my hands up and down her thighs before gripping them. The music coming from my speaker caught my attention when I heard D'Angelo come on.

"I want some of your brown sugar," I sang against her lips. I continued to hum the words while kissing her neck.

Shiloh was my brown sugar.

Sweet, addictive, and she provided me with a high I hadn't felt since I was a young boy running wild trying to ignore the grief I was feeling after losing my mother. Last night, Shi and I talked more about our pasts. It felt good to be candid about my feelings and not fear judgment or worse, pity. Shi was able to empathize and was open about her estranged relationship with her father.

When she was a teenager, she and her mother had a rough relationship after she learned the truth about her father's sudden disappearance. And even into adulthood, their relationship suffered. Every man she dated was like her father unavailable and selfish. At five in the morning wrapped in one another, we learned we both were grieving the loss of our parents. My mother passed when I was fourteen and her father stopped coming around when she was just ten years old.

I could never understand how a man could abandon his responsibilities as a father. My Pops and I had our issues, but no matter what he never turned his back on me.

Ever.

The loss of my mother changed our relationship, he was grieving just as much as my sister and me. But he was forced to put his feelings on the back burner to make sure we were good. He even had to deal with the thirsty women from the church that couldn't wait to take my mother's place as the first lady.

"What are you thinking about?" Shi asked.

"Life."

She hummed before rubbing small circles on my back. We went back to listening to my playlist until I got a call that interrupted our vibe. She grabbed my phone from the table and handed it to me then took our plates to the kitchen.

"What's up, Pops?" I said after answering his face-time call.

"Just checking in, son."

Looking at my Pops was like getting a glimpse of what I'd look like in 30 years. The only major difference was our eyes. My mother blessed me and my sister with her intense gray eyes, whereas, Pops eyes were honey-brown. He's always kept his hair cut low and goatee cut low. It gave him a polished look.

"I'm good. How's everybody down there?"

"We're good. Getting everything together for my anniversary next month. You know your sister is running around here trying to make sure everything is *perfect*."

"Monica is just like mom a true perfectionist," I said with a chuckle.

Pops smiled at the mention of my mother. Unlike me, he loved to talk about her. There were so many stories he had about her and us that it never got old. They'd known each other their whole life, grew up in my grandfather's church together, and even went to college together before finally getting married. Their story was truly one of a kind.

Once in a lifetime.

Their love was something I wanted.

"So, what will be the weekend of events?" I asked before walking toward the kitchen where Shi was washing dishes.

"Fish Fry on Friday, Family Day/Carnival on Saturday, and on Sunday we will have our regular service followed by dinner."

I nodded. "Sounds like a plan, I'll see you then."

"You bringing anyone?"

"I might." I looked at Shi who stopped rinsing a glass and looked at me. "I'll talk to you tomorrow, Pops. Love you."

"Love you too, son."

Once Pops hung up, I placed my phone on the island and walked over to Shi. I grabbed her by the waist turning her around. She leaned against the sink her hands covered in suds. When she started chewing on her bottom lip, I leaned down and kissed her forehead, then her cheek.

"A lot can happen in a month, you know?" she whispered.

"I know."

"And you want me to go with you to your father's pastoral anniversary?"

The apprehension she felt was all over her face. Seeing her flustered was cute. Letting go of her waist, I walked over to the paper towels and ripped off two sheets for her. When she finished drying her hands, I picked her up and sat on the island. I stood between her legs with both hands planted firmly beside her.

"This isn't going to be a short-term thing for me."

She raised her brow then she flashed that innocent smile I was growing to like more and more.

"Oh yeah?" She leaned back on her hands and twisted her lips.

"Do you feel the same way?"

"Yes."

"Good. Now put on your dress from last night so we can go to the store and get you some clothes for the weekend."

"What?"

"You're mine for the weekend, love."

"I like the sound of that," she said against my lips.

***

"Where are you taking me?" she asked while pushing out a breath.

I looked back at and smiled. She was dressed comfortably in a hoodie and a pair of leggings. The Chuck Taylor's she wore wasn't the best choice for the adventure I had in mind, but they were what she wanted. Her hair was pulled into a low ponytail and was covered by one of my hats.

Every Saturday morning, I ran this trail until I reached the creek at the end. The fresh air and the sound of the water were soothing. It brought me peace, I spent my time here either meditating or just enjoying the scenery.

"We're almost there, love."

When we reached the end of the trail, there were boulders to our right where I led us and took a seat. She looked at the creek with wide eyes. I knew she'd appreciate this view just as much as I did.

"I come here after my morning runs. Didn't have the chance to come this morning though." She looked at me and started blushing.

"It's beautiful. How did you find this place?" She looked up at the sun peeking through the tall trees. The sound of the water and the birds chirping echoed through the air.

"Ran off the original trail and ended up here. This has been my route ever since. Even come here at night every now and again. I come here and talk to my mom sometimes. This is the type of stuff she liked."

Shi reached for my hand and gripped it. We sat in silence and took in all the creek had to offer us. Roseville was filled with gems and I looked forward to finding them all. While Shi took pictures, I secretly took a few of her. We stayed until the sun started to set. On our way back to my place, I heard her stomach growling and we both laughed.

"Let's go to our spot," she said.

"Oh, we got a spot now?" I teased while throwing my arm over her shoulder. She nodded and interlocked her fingers with mine as we continued our stroll.

Once we reached *Over Easy*, we were greeted by Mimi and her beautiful smile.

"Missed you last night," she said while walking us to our table. "But now I see why you didn't show up."

After Shi and I sat down, she stood at the table with her hands on her hips. The look on her face was one I couldn't read. Knowing Mimi, she was going to share what she was thinking.

"What's on your mind?" I asked looking at her then Shi.

"I like this." She pointed between me and Shi. "I want to see more of it."

"Oh, you will." I looked at Shi and winked. Shi kept her attention on me while nodding with a lusty look in her eye that made me want to skip dinner.

Yeah, Mimi was definitely going to see more of Shi and me around here.

EPILOGUE

One month later...

I WAS NERVOUS.

Actually, I was beyond nervous. Marq looked at me and smiled as he pulled into his father's driveway. When he placed his hand on my leg, I calmed down a bit, but the nerves were still there. We'd driven all the way from D.C. to Lithonia for his father's 25th pastoral anniversary. I was slightly embarrassed to admit that I'd grown up as one of those people who only attended church two maybe three times a year, but Marq reassured me his father and sister wouldn't judge me.

The hardest part of our journey –spending the night in Richmond– was over. Since Marq felt so strongly about me meeting his family, it felt right to introduce him to my mother. Surprisingly, Mama and Marq hit it off. She was nice to him completely negating all the things I'd told him she would do.

It shocked me how well she treated him even going as far as showing him my embarrassing baby pictures. Seeing them interact was refreshing. It would've been hard for her to be mean to him. Marq was like a light and he had brightened my life ever since the night we hung out.

In just a month he'd made my life better. I'd grown accustomed to our little routine that included dates *at Over E*asy and walks to the creek. He was truly a night owl, consistently keeping me up until the sun rose. My weekends belonged to him now and from Monday to Thursday, I counted down the minutes until I'd be back in his arm*s*.

I had it bad.

"You ready," he asked after parking. With a nod, I unbuckled my seatbelt and opened the door.

The carnival was in full swing by the time we arrived. It was set up just like the many carnival's I'd attended as a kid. Booths for games, food stations, and even a petting zoo filled the grassy fields Monica rented for the day. Children were running around with cotton candy and balloons in hand, it was a beautiful sight.

Monica, Marq's sister, spotted us and waved for us to come to her. Marq gripped my hand tighter as he led us to her. The smile on his face warmed my heart. I knew how much he missed his family. He's been talking about this trip non-stop. Monica was manning the ice cream cart next to the whack-a-mole booth. She looked exactly like the photos Marq had shown me.

When we finally reached her, she grabbed me and

hugged me like she'd known me for years. Her hug felt familiar and genuine. I had no choice but to reciprocate.

"So nice to finally meet you in person, pretty." She and I stood eye to eye. Her hair was curly and wild with honey blonde highlights throughout. The freckles on her cheeks and nose were more noticeable than the pictures I'd seen. She was absolutely gorgeous. Just like their mother.

"Can I get some love too, Mo?" Marq asked after watching our lengthy exchange.

"Still a spoiled baby," she teased while hugging him.

I stepped back and watched them hug. I'd always wondered what it was like to have siblings. What it felt like to know someone would always have your back no matter what happened. I grew up with a slew of cousins, but as we got older, we drifted apart. The stories Marq shared about he and Monica made the yearning to reconnect grow.

He encouraged me to get close with them again and to reach out to my half-siblings even if my relationship with my father was nonexistent. That was one thing I loved about Marq, he remained positive no matter what. Thanks to him and social media I was able to find my older sister, Laura and younger brother, Solomon Jr. Our relationship was still in the beginning stages, but it was an optimistic start.

While Marq and Monica continued to catch up, I noticed their father coming over. He and Marq looked a lot more alike than I thought. He swaggered over in a cream linen suit a brown fedora and matching shoes.

"You must be Shiloh?" He wrapped his arms around me in an embrace I couldn't begin to explain.

"Nice to meet you, Pastor Kent."

He looked at me and smiled. "We're family, you call me Pops."

Everything Marq told me about his father and sister being warm and receptive people, remained true. I stepped aside so Marq and his father could catch up. Monica offered me an ice cream cone and I gladly accepted. The sundress I wore wasn't doing much in keeping me cool in this Georgia sun.

Watching Marq talk to his childhood friends and church family was something I didn't think I'd enjoy as much as I did. I was seated at a picnic table enjoying my food while he conversed and took pictures. Every now and then, he'd look my way and smile. After an hour or so of catching up with people, he found his way back to me. He threw his leg over the bench and pulled me between his legs.

"I missed you," he whispered in my ear. I fell into his embrace and shook my head at how quickly I was falling for him. But like he always said love has no timeframe

"I've been here this whole time. No way you missed me."

I turned to him and the serious look in his eyes made my smile drop.

"Thank you for coming."

My smile returned at the sight of his. "Thank you for inviting me. I didn't expect to have as much fun as I am." I pointed to my empty plate. "And the food is better than I imagined."

He grabbed my hand and kissed it before interlocking his fingers with mine.

"Come on, let's go play some games so I can win that stuffed animal I saw you eyeing when we first got here."

*I guess Ellie w*as right, my Prince Charming was closer than I thought.

THE END...

THANK YOU!

Thank you for taking the time to read **brown sugar**. I kindly ask that you consider leaving a review on Amazon and Goodreads!

Xoxo,
D.

ACKNOWLEDGMENTS

God, for this gift!

***Teon,** for allowing me to use your poetry and prose.

Tamara, you are everything!

Bria, for your feedback and pep talks!

Family and friends, for you alls unwavering support!

*Poetry used in this novella comes from the anthology **"Joy Comes in The Morning,"** it can be read/purchased **on Amazon.com**

ALSO BY D. ROSE

**Intro to Nina & Mecca:*

New Year Kiss (A Short Story)

Second Chance Series:

Another Chance to Love

All I Need is You

Your Love Series:

Yearning for Your Love

Standalone Titles:

Cherie Amour

Made in the USA
Columbia, SC
27 April 2020